Carrying the Cross and Following Jesus:
The significance and art of bearing our crosses

Carrying the Cross and Following Jesus:

The significance and art of bearing our crosses

Paul Chungath

2018

Carrying the Cross and Following Jesus: *The Significance and art of bearing our crosses* — published by the Rev. Dr. Ashish Amos of the Indian Society for Promoting Christian Knowledge (ISPCK), Post Box 1585, Kashmere Gate, Delhi-110006.

© Author, 2018

Online order: http://ispck.org.in/book.php

Also available on amazon.in

ISBN: 978-81-8465-664-0

Cover design: Fr. James Kadavy

Laser typeset by

ISPCK, Post Box 1585, 1654, Madarsa Road, Kashmere Gate, Delhi-110006 • *Tel:* 23866323

e-mail: ashish@ispck.org.in • ella@ispck.org.in
website: www.ispck.org.in

Contents

Foreword ... *vii*

Preface ... *xi*

Introduction ... *xiii*

1. Meaning and types of the cross ... 1

   1.1. Meaning of the cross ... 1

   1.2. Types of crosses ... 4

2. Significance of the cross ... 7

   2.1. Essentiality of the cross for discipleship ... 8

   2.2. Essentiality of the cross for Eternal Life ... 12

   2.3. Purification of soul to be perfect ... 17

   2.4. Sign of God's love for us ... 19

   2.5. Effectiveness of prayer with the cross ... 22

   2.6. The cross produces perseverance ... 25

   2.7. Life-giving source ... 27

   2.8. Merits promised by Jesus ... 29

   2.9. Humility ... 32

Contents

2.10.	Share holder in salvation economy	...	34
2.11.	More intimacy with God	...	36
2. 12.	Maturity and fruitfulness	...	38
3.	The art bearing our crosses	...	41
3.1.	Acceptance and total surrender	...	42
3.2.	Enable the cross to bear fruit	...	44
3.3.	Importance of Gethsemane	...	47
3.4.	Praying for the cross	...	49
3.5.	Carrying Jesus along and faith in His presence	...	51
3.6.	Child like trust in God	...	54
3.7.	Holy Eucharist and its continuity in daily life	...	57
3.8.	Contemplation on the sufferings of Jesus	...	60
3.9.	Wise and mature spiritual director	...	62
3.10.	Ascetical practices	...	64
3.11.	Bearing it for the love of Jesus	...	66
3.12.	Praise and thanksgiving	...	69
Conclusion		...	72
Other books of the same author		...	75

Foreword

Fr. Paul wanted me to write a foreword for his book: "Carrying the Cross and following Jesus". I was not too well and so I thought I won't be able to read the book and prepare the foreword. Later, when I felt better, I decided to read a few pages of the book. And believe me, I could not stop reading: I read the whole book. People who are going to read this book, I guess, would appreciate kind of evaluation of the book. I would have loved to do that, high - lighting some of the more important and striking points in the book, but I was at a loss what to do because I found the whole booklet so rich, spiritual and scriptural and appropriately backed by saints, that there was nothing in the book that could be side tracked. Going through the book I felt that the book was a creation of a person who has himself carried the cross and put into practice the advice he has for the readers.

I am writing these lines in the Holy Week. My eyes are fixed on the Resurrection of the Lord, but the words of 'Angelus' resound in my heart "that we may, by his passion and cross be brought to the glory of His resurrection". Cross is no more a punishment and ignominy, but the path to Resurrection and Glory. "If anyone wishes to come after me, he must deny himself and take up his cross daily and follow me" said Jesus: [Luke 9:13] his words are clear: All have crosses to bear. Jesus did not say, he must take up his cross if he has any. Yes, all do have. Our life's journey is a way of the cross. You may be wondering what these crosses might be. Fr. Paul enumerates a few: sickness, disability, poverty, inconveniences, contradictions, misunderstanding, false accusations, and painful experiences of our life, mental or physical. For Jesus, carrying the cross is not something optional, but an essential requirement to be a disciple. Jesus carried the cross himself [John 19; 17] accepting the will of the Father, for our salvation. Now he is expecting each of us to do our share for our salvation by carrying our own cross.

So we have our crosses and we have to carry. These statements might smack of kind of sadism. Fr. Paul alerts us to divest ourselves of any such concept. He wants us to know that the cross put on us by the Lord is a sign of his love for us. He brings forward the testimony of great saints to support this statement. Beyond these personal advantages that we gain through bearing the cross, there is of course the great role we play namely the sharing of the sufferings of Christ. "We fill up in our bodies whatever is wanting in the suffering of Christ". Colossus 1:24. Our suffering becomes the suffering of Christ; they assume a Christic dimension that embraces all humankind.

The cross is a precious rose but has hidden thorns. To make the pain of the thorn less painful Fr. Paul suggests a few methods under the title "The art of bearing the cross". Fr. Paul says, when our mental setup is positively attuned towards the daily cross, the weight of the cross diminishes psychologically, even though the physical heaviness of the cross remains the same.

A previous mind-set can also be helpful to face the crosses and trials more effectively. A surprise visit of a friend, for example, may find us unprepared or lead us to an embarrassing situation: but an expected visit and well prepared reception will surely be comfortable. So it is with crosses too.

Another beautiful advice of Fr. Paul: Take Jesus along with you, wherever you go, whatever you do, feeling his presence dialoguing with him through short prayers. Be sure, you will be strengthened to face your crosses squarely.

Fr. Paul's book, in short, explains what the cross is, its meaning, its inevitability, necessity, and its importance in spiritual life. The cross that seems unpalatable can become delightful if only we discover the love that moulds it to suit each bearer. When I bear the cross I am immediately in the company of Jesus who tells, me, you bear your cross daily and follow me.

Fr. Paul has enriched us with a beautiful book, let us hope more such books, will follow. God bless him, and his devoted readers.

Mar Jacob Thoomkuzhy

Abp. em. of Trichur

Preface

This is a revised edition of my previous book with the same title published in 2015, during the years of consecrated life, in Shanti Ashram. Few sub titles are added and some matter modified and as per the reader's request.

I express my profound gratitude to His Grace Mar Jacob Thoomkuzhy, Abp. Em. of Trichur for the foreword. I gratefully remember Rev. Sr. Sabina Sequeira CSSJ and Ruth Henderson O.P. who patiently went through and corrected the material. I am thankful to ISPCK, Delhi, for their readiness to publish this book.

Certain readers of this book may misunderstand our God as a sadist wondering whether Jesus was 'sadistic' in his teaching. My intention is certainly not to picture God in a negative way. God doesn't enjoy the suffering of His creatures. We have to accept that human beings are imperfect and not equal to God. Sufferings are inherent in the process of perfection and to gain eternal life. Secondly, it is the law of nature that in order to achieve something, one has to go through the process of suffering; no pain no gain. Jesus the Son of God, himself had to undergo severe unjust suffering and death on the Cross for the ransom of humanity.

Introduction

There is an innate tendency in human beings to avoid sufferings, which the cross symbolizes and to lean towards comforts. The major part of human prayer is to get relief from suffering. Many of us pray only in times of suffering. Some consider prayer only as requesting God for a better life; in other words, relief from pain, sickness, inconveniences etc. Therefore our desires and prayers are oriented to avoid the cross of suffering. Hence wiping out the "suffering" aspect is a great human concern. Naturally, the majority of people are fully occupied in this attempt regarding their own life, although some, indeed, are concerned to remove the suffering of others. In the midst of this struggle to avoid the cross of suffering, it is essential to know the indispensable need of suffering for one's salvation and eternal life. Thus perfection of the human being, and also the means to the final goal of our earthly voyage, involves suffering. A Chinese proverb rightly puts it "The diamond cannot be polished without friction, nor the man perfected without trials and pain".

Even though Jesus prayed in the garden of Gethsemane to his Heavenly Father to take away the cup of suffering which was to come on his way, in the concluding part of the same prayer he surrendered to the Will of God. Both human nature and divine nature can be seen in Jesus' prayer at Gethsemane. In the attempt to avoid the suffering, he presented his human nature and his divine nature as visible in the willingness to take up the cross, as the will of God to save humanity.

Suffering is there in the bearing up of the same and experienced even after. Heaviness is experienced in both stages of bearing the fruit. This is true in the case of any being on earth. The process of bearing fruit has to involve sufferings. As we know, the trees which have fruits get more stones thrown at them than the fruitless trees. This phenomenon can be seen in the case of human life. Whoever does something for the betterment of the society has to face more criticism and persecution than non doers. In other words one has to struggle to bear fruit, and struggle to survive.

This book is a humble attempt to highlight the significance of the cross and the art of bearing it in our lives. It's meant especially for those who are intending to follow Jesus and his ways in order to attain eternal life. There are

3 major aspects dealt with in this work: 1) Meaning and types of crosses, 2) Significance of the cross and 3) The art of bearing our crosses.

> *Let us understand that God is a physician, and that suffering is a medicine for salvation, not a punishment for damnation.*
>
> — St. Augustine

1

Meaning and types of the cross

1.1.   Meaning of the cross

The term "cross" can have various meanings according to the mindset or imagination of a person. During the earthly life of Jesus Christ, the cross was a tool of punishment of criminals for the Jews, thus a symbol with a negative meaning. In the modern world a non believer in Christ wears a cross like a locket around the neck. A bad character in the films, the 'villain' or hero sometimes has a cross around the neck. But for a true Christian the Cross is a sacred symbol, since Jesus Christ, Son of God, died on the cross. For the followers of Christ, the Cross is a sign of salvation. In the words of St. Paul "For the word of cross is folly to those who are perishing, but to us who are being saved it is the power of God" (1 Cor. 1:18). The image of the cross also brings to the mind of the Christian user and to the onlookers a Christian presence in the place where it is seen. Thus today places of worship, institutions and even houses of Christians are well recognized by this sign of the cross. These are all external meanings of the cross, which brings the Suffering Jesus to the mind of a person who comes into contact with it. But there is, more importantly, an internal and theological meaning, which is the suffering aspect, that Jesus expected from his followers and disciples that they may attain an eternal reward after their earthly pilgrimage. St. Gregory writes, "It is so wise of God to allow the time of this pilgrimage to be full of trials. The present is only a path to our eternal home."

In this book when we use the term "Cross", the emphasis is on its internal or theological meaning i.e. suffering for a better cause. We are not concerned about its physical nature or secular meaning.

"Whoever wishes to follow me let him deny himself, take up his cross and follow me" (Mt. 16:24). Carrying one's own cross is an indispensable condition put forward by Jesus to his followers. "Woe to him," cries St. Bernard, "who carries not his own cross, but another". Many find satisfaction in meditating upon the passion of Jesus Christ, emotionally participating in the way of the cross, weeping in front of Jesus' Cross, wearing a crucifix, medal etc. These pious practices will not suffice to answer the demand of Jesus to carry one's own cross. Such pious practices will certainly help us to remember the sufferings of Jesus while carrying his cross. But each one of us has to carry her/his own cross in order to fulfill the demand of discipleship and enter into the eternal reward. The cross can be in the form sickness, disability, poverty, inconveniences, contradictions, misunderstandings, false accusations etc. In other words all painful experiences of our life, whether mental or physical, can be considered as the cross given to us.

On the Way of the Cross, you see, my children, only the first step is painful. Our greatest cross is the fear of crosses. . .We have not the courage to carry our cross, and we are very much mistaken; for, whatever we do, the cross holds us tight -- we cannot escape from it. What, then, have we to lose? Why not love our crosses, and make use of them to take us to heaven?

— St. John Mary Vianney

1.2. Types of crosses

There are four types of crosses and all the crosses can profit a person, if one carries them with the right attitude. Whether it becomes profitable or not depends on each person who bears it. The types of crosses according to the sources can be classified in the following ways:-

1.   Willed by God

There are sufferings in our life, originating not from human or other beings of the world but of unknown origin and, we consider them as willed by God. In this category come various kinds of sufferings, such as deformities and sickness by birth, natural calamities, and atrocities.

2.   From other beings

There are sufferings which come from other beings either human or animal. Here too there are two categories, namely intentional or non-intentional. Accidents, attacks, physical and mental torturing, false accusations etc. can be considered in this category.

3.   From one's own mistake

sufferings can originate from one's own mistakes. Under this category come accidents, loss of goods and various sicknesses, due to one's own careless life.

4. From one's choice

Sufferings also can be taken as of one's own choice. Here we can include voluntary sufferings taken in the form of sacrifices for one's own purification and salvation.

> *If God gives you an abundant harvest of trials, it is a sign of great holiness which He desires you to attain. Do you want to become a great saint? Ask God to send you many sufferings.*
>
> — Saint Ignatius of Loyola

Know, There Is A Way

When darkness comes and fear fills your heart,
Know, there is a way.

When all your dreams come crashing down,
Know there is a way.

When friends cannot be found
and there is No one to comfort you,
Know there is a way.

When you are ready to lay down and quit,
Know there is a way.

To know, is to find the way.
Knowing cannot be found "out there".

Knowing is found in the silence
Of surrender within.
The Way is within.

– John McIntosh and Rev. JoAnn Polito

2

Significance of the cross

Suffering has meaning and purpose in the life of human beings. Suffering has great potential. In the history of salvation no suffering is a waste. The story of Joseph in the Old Testament is a proof of this potentiality of suffering. The Israelites experienced unprecedented manifestation of God's amazing love and care during their 40 years of hardships in the desert.

Knowledge of the significance of a challenge in our life will ease our burden in facing it. This is true in the case of our daily crosses willed by God for our betterment. The importance of our daily sufferings can be explained in twelve ways in relation to their usefulness for us.

2.1. Essentiality of the cross for discipleship

Jesus taught his disciples and people of his time about the essentiality of the cross in order to be his disciples or followers. His words from Scripture verify this: "take up their cross and follow me" (Mt. 16:24; Mk.8:34). "He who does not take his cross and follow me is not worthy of me" (Mt. 10:38). "Take up your cross daily and follow me" (Lk. 9:23). "Whoever does not bear his own cross cannot be my disciple" (Lk. 14:27). It is common understanding that discipleship demands the following of the Master.

From the above scripture references it is clear that following Jesus requires sacrifices. The need to sacrifice one's own familial relationship to be his disciples is expressed in the following words of Jesus: "If any one comes to me and does not hate his own father and mother and wife and children and brothers and sisters, yes, and even his own life, he cannot be my disciple" (Lk. 14:26). Jesus made it very clear that sacrificing one's own comfort and family bonds are essential conditions to be his disciples (cfr. Mt. 8:19-22). The term 'follow me' used by Jesus, meant doing as He did and imitating His ways. Jesus took his own cross (Jn. 19:17) fulfilling the will of the Heavenly Father and as his share for the salvation of all humanity. And now he is expecting each one of us to do our share for our salvation, that is, carrying one's cross.

Suffering is a remarkable sign that indicates a person is walking in the footsteps of Jesus. "It is commendable if someone bears up under the pain of unjust suffering, because they are conscious of God. ... If you suffer for doing good and you endure it, this is commendable before God. To this you were called, because Christ suffered for you, leaving you an example, that you should follow in his steps" (1 Peter 2:19-21).

Traditionally there were various means both for penance and also to be close followers of Jesus such as wearing a hair shirt, pricking chains round the waist, and beating oneself to imitate the scourging of Jesus etc. In the modern world even among professed religious these practices are vanishing. But there are various occasions in our life when we may imitate the suffering Jesus and receive the effect of penance. It is the taking up of difficult moments patiently and bearing all kinds of suffering with the attitude of penance and offered for the love of our crucified Jesus. In this manner saints accepted their daily cross and reached their final victory.

Naturally one may easily cling to the comforts and joyful matters in following Jesus and keep aside or ignore the harder portions. At the time of the multiplication of bread many were there with Jesus, but at the time of His suffering and death on the cross, these crowds abandoned Him. This phenomenon is occurring in the modern followers of Jesus. St. Theresa Margret wrote, "Remember that when you entered religion, you proposed to express in yourself the life of the crucified." It is a fact that ordination for priests or first profession for religious is not the culmination of one's vocation. It is only going half way and the rest is the toughest part – to be a saint. As Jesus prayed at Gethsemane, all consecrated people need a Gethsemane experience in order to face the daily cross.

Painful experiences or trials that come in our daily life as our crosses enable us to share Christ's suffering – the chalice of suffering given to his disciples to drink. Jesus said to James and John "can you drink the cup I am to drink?" and their answer was "yes" and this was approved by Jesus. Most of his disciples were martyred and the early Christian community had to undergo persecution for the fact of being the followers of Jesus. St. Peter encouraged the Christians of his time to face suffering for the love of Jesus and participate in Christ's suffering. "Dear friends, do not be surprised at the fiery ordeal that has come on you to test you, as though something strange were happening to you. But rejoice inasmuch as you participate in the sufferings of Christ, so that you may be overjoyed when his glory is revealed" (1 Peter 4:12-13).

> *Contradictions — there is a really sharp hair shirt! There is a penance which has made saints, and which everyone can practice!*
>
> — St. Frances Xavier Cabrini

2.2. Essentiality of the cross for Eternal Life

Bearing the cross of suffering is considered to be an essential element to gain eternal life. This is crystal clear in

the teachings of Christ. While teaching on the necessity of carrying one's daily cross to be his disciples, he added that this way of self denial and bearing the cross is also essential to have eternal life (cfr. Mt. 16:24-27). Jesus Christ, Son of God, came to this world to give eternal life for many (cfr. Jn. 3:16), in other words to save mankind. In his salvific plan carrying the cross is an essential element to gain

eternal life, from which he himself was not spared in the plan of God the Father. The basic element in the teachings of Jesus with regard to eternal life can be summed up in one sentence; without bearing the cross no one can enter into heaven. There are various scriptural references to utterances of Jesus with regard to the Kingdom of Heaven or eternal life, for example, the Bible passages Mt.16:24-27; Mt.10:38-39; Mk. 8:34.

Renunciation of worldly comfort

Voluntary sacrifice and discomfort, a form of the cross, to attain eternal life, is also proposed by Jesus to a young man in the Gospel according to St. Mathew, and to the ruler in St. Luke's version (cfr. Mt. 19:16-30; cfr. Lk. 18:18-30). Here the question was, "What shall I do to have eternal life?" The answer of Jesus was very radical and hard to practice; 'Sell all that you have and give to the poor' (Mt. 19:21; Lk. 18: 22). It is a difficult task to leave the property built up by one's own hard work. In the parable of the rich man and Lazarus the reason for the rich man's misfortune after death as pointed out by Abraham is not his immoral life but the luxurious life he led in the world. "Son, remember that you in your life time received your good things, and Lazarus in like manner evil things; but now he is comforted here, and you are in anguish" (Lk 16:25). St. John Chrysostom says; "When you see a man leading an evil life not suffering at all, do not imagine that he is happy, but rather weep and mourn that, he will have to suffer so much hereafter. On the other hand when you see a virtuous man afflicted, consider him to be fortunate, because he will have atoned for all his sins on earth, and like Lazarus can look forward to a great reward."

Certainly voluntary sacrifice and discomfort in one's life can be the means to attain eternal life. In this way a person pays the cost of eternal life by accepting willingly the renunciation of worldly comfort. Jesus taught us 'Sell everything to get the treasure of the Kingdom of God' (Mt. 13; 44-46). According to St. Mark the Ascetic "He who enjoys bodily pleasures beyond the proper limit will pay for the excess a hundredfold in sufferings".

Invitation to enter through the narrow gate

Suffering and hardship

There are various themes of Jesus' teaching indicating this fact; 'Enter through the narrow gate' (Mt. 7:13-14; Lk. 13:23-24), 'blessed are those who are persecuted for righteousness' (Mt. 5:10; Lk. 6:22), 'Persecution for my sake' (Mt. 5:11-12) and 'Unless a grain of wheat fall on earth can't bear fruit' (cfr. Jn. 12:24). We all have to undergo the same process of a grain of wheat to produce fruit; fruit of our earthly pilgrimage towards the heavenly abode. It is in this spirit St. Therese of Child Jesus wrote in her letter to a missionary "Brother it is indeed more through suffering and persecution than through eloquent preaching, that God wills to establish His kingdom in souls."

Doing the will of God and following God's commandments though it is hard

Some of Jesus' disciples left because of the hardness of his teaching (cfr. Jn. 6:66). Even in modern times the majority of Jesus' followers remain nominal Christians because it is hard to practice His teachings word by word. Some left Christianity and became atheists or entered other religions, whereas some others remained partially following the teachings of Christ. Jesus taught that it is not enough to say 'Lord, Lord but one must do the will of God to enter into eternal life' (Mt. 7:21; Lk. 6:46-49). This requires sacrifice and a painful undertaking, and on certain occasions, is very hard to practice.

It is good to have sufficiently paid our debts here on earth through bearing the daily cross before starting our heavenly journey. Some become conscious of the need for this payment at the evening hours of their life span and others on their death bed. Then they try their best to pay the rest through repentance and proper penance. Since we do not know the exact time of our final journey to the heavenly abode, it is better not to keep any payment for the eleventh hour, rather pay it on a daily basis.

"We can really go to Heaven through suffering" says St. Vincent De Paul "but it is not all those who suffer who find salvation. It is only those who suffer readily for the love of Jesus, who first suffered for us". When St. Ludwic, was seriously ill for 28 years, she saw in a vision the crown which had been prepared for her in heaven. It was very beautiful, but not complete. She prayed to our Lord Jesus to complete it. Then, cruel soldiers entered, who struck her and abused her. Later an angel appeared to her and told her that the action of the soldiers completed her crown in heaven. According to St. John Mary Vianney, "Contradictions bring us to the foot of the cross, and the cross to the gate of heaven". In the view of St. Cyprian, "Sufferings are the wings by which all climb to heaven".

> *If there be a true way that leads to the everlasting Kingdom, it is most certainly that of suffering, patiently endured.*
>
> – St. Colette

2.3. Purification of soul to be perfect

Through suffering a sinner is purified, St. Margaret Mary writes, "The sanctity of God's justice was imprinted on my soul in a manner so terrible, that I was ready to accept every kind of suffering, and sacrifice myself for damned souls, rather than appear before that Holiness with a single stain on my soul."

From the biographies of saints we can understand that they have undergone several dark nights or moments of suffering. They were convinced that these experiences of sufferings or dark nights purify one's soul in the way of perfection. Understanding this fact they joyfully accepted the suffering, submitted themselves for purification and reached their final goal.

It is better to have purified ourselves here on earth in order to get a full ticket to heaven. A half paid ticket in our earthly span of life leaves the rest to be paid in purgatory, the place before heaven. We might have noticed in the train, the ticket examiner collects money from the travelers who did not pay the latest increase of the ticket fare and only then permits them to travel on. The fact of an unpurified life will not make one eligible to enter the heavenly abode; instead the life is left in between, and one is forcefully made to pay the rest. This can be verified from the parable of Jesus in the form of the answer of Abraham to the rich man "Son, remember that you in your lifetime received your good things, and Lazarus in like manner evil things; but now he is comforted here, and you are in anguish"(Lk.16:25). This parable of Jesus gives sufficient proof about the necessity of purification by suffering the cross on earth, in order to reach heaven.

> *Contradictions, sickness, scruples, spiritual dryness, and interior or exterior torments are but the chisel which God uses to carve his statues for paradise.*
>
> – St. Alphonsus De Ligouri

2.4. Sign of God's love for us

Our crosses in the form of sufferings are to be considered as the sign of God's love for us. To those whom He loves, he sends sufferings to purify and enable them to reach eternal life. Whoever has suffered enough and been purified sufficiently is taken to heaven, while others are sent for further purification in purgatory. When a person is not purified well within the given time of life before death, God sometimes sends serious and painful sickness. In some cases a person is bedridden for a long time. I believe this is

the sign of God's love for that person as He wishes to purify him/her thoroughly on earth itself and take the person soon to heaven. On the other hand some people who die without proper purification are given a chance to be purified in purgatory. I strongly believe that without proper purification none can be taken to heaven. If that is so, it is better we submit ourselves in the hands of God to be purified during our earthly life span itself, without murmur and complaint, accepting sufferings cheerfully. It is also possible to try to voluntarily accept or request sufferings in order to be purified. When we go through the life history of saints we can find that the Saints who suffered intense sufferings, voluntarily or given by God, went earlier to heaven. Some came on the track very late but they ran the race towards perfection in purification quickly and reached their goal, even before the person who started the race early.

St. Therese of Child Jesus wrote to her sister, Sr. Celine when their father was struck by the terrible disease: "Jesus presents us with the cross, a heavy cross indeed. What a privilege for us! How He must love us to send us such a great sorrow. Aren't we worthy of being envied?" We do not have a complete choice of our life span and mode of suffering because we are like clay in the hands of a potter. The Potter has freedom to take first which part of the clay he wishes, to make pots and also to choose the kind of pots. The clay has to surrender itself into the hands of the potter. Thus there are differences in the sufferings and duration of sufferings designed by God. "But who are you, a man, to answer back to God? Will what is moulded say to its moulder, 'Why have you made me thus?' Has the potter no right over the clay, to make out of the same lump one vessel for beauty and another for menial use?" (Rom. 9:20-21).

"Let us not believe', says St. John Chrysostom, "that trials are a sign that God has either forgotten or despised us; on the contrary, let us regard them rather as an indication that

God occupies Himself with us, seeking to purify us from our sins. With this assurance, let us not give way to sadness in the midst of our trials, but rejoice with St. Paul, 'I rejoice in my trials.' The highest degree of fortitude is displayed by the soul who gives thanks for the trial". "Suffering in body and soul is proof of union of God with the soul" Jesus to St. Gertrude.

> *The love of Jesus is made manifest in the crosses that he gives to you. To the ones he loves more, he gives more crosses and trials. Literally I love suffering and a day that goes without any suffering is a day lost.*
>
> — St. Alphonsa

2.5. Effectiveness of prayer with the cross

Jesus' place of prayer was usually on mountains neither in comfortable places nor in the Jerusalem temple, though he used to go there on feast days. Jesus' prayer at Gethsemane was kneeling down on a stone in the open air, sweating blood, sacrificing the night's sleep. The praying gesture of Jesus' prayer on the cross is the greatest prayer; a sacrifice and prayer with physical pain to save the whole of mankind, the best form of prayer, a prayer for a great need indeed!

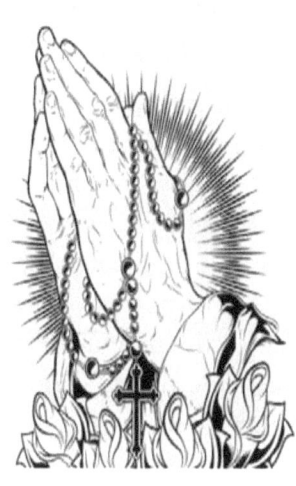

"Take a comfortable posture", is the dictum heard from those who start leading a guided meditation. Creating a comfortable atmosphere leads to a maximum removal of roughness from the sitting, kneeling and even walking places; sponge sheets are placed under soft, costly carpets. There are cushions on sitting places and even at the back to lean on. The kneeler is furnished with sponge cushions etc. Some followers of Christ go even further, using air conditioned rooms, well-furnished and decorated rooms with costly elements.

This gives the prayer place the look of a palace instead of a Church or chapel. As a whole, a totally comfortable posture in prayer is created but this results in reaching far away from the spirit of Jesus who prayed surrounded by total discomfort. Comfort seeking even contradicts Jesus' teachings: "Enter by the narrow gate . . . find it are few" (Mt.7:13-14).

The more discomfort, the greater will be the effect in our prayers. We need to pay higher to get greater things and also make it faster in achieving the goal. When we pay more we can purchase better quality materials. Paying more we can use faster means of conveyance to reach our destination. Once Jesus' disciples tried with ordinary means of prayer to cure an epileptic boy, but failed. Jesus explained the reason for their failure, saying that prayer with fasting is needed to cure such a sickness. It indicates that prayer with sacrifice gives better effects. Jesus spent forty days and nights in prayer and he was strengthened to defeat Satan who approached Him with temptations. Again prayer with discomfort and agony enabled him to get strength and courage to face death on the cross. Sacrificing the comfortable posture and taking up discomfort and a painful posture, will give better results in our prayers. For example prayer while kneeling down on stone pieces or metal would give comparatively better results than sitting on cushions. Kneeling on the rough surface on stones in prayer can be for three intentions; 1) prayer to be heard quickly 2) for a greater need; 3) to reduce one's future torments in purgatory.

Growing up in the love of Jesus, St. Rose of Lima once had a vision. An angel brought two crowns – one with flowers and the other with thorns – and asked her to choose one of them. The angel said "Whatever you choose will be pleasing to Jesus." She chose the thorny crown saying, "My bridegroom is wearing a thorny crown on the cross, how can I wear a flowery crown?"

I am better pleased with your intentions which you offer when in a state of suffering, than with sweetness of your devotion which gives pleasure to yourself.

– Jesus to St. Gertrude

2.6. The cross produces perseverance

The cross produces perseverance, character and hope. "We also glory in our sufferings, because we know that suffering produces perseverance; perseverance, character; and character, hope. And hope does not put us to shame, because God's love has been poured out into our hearts through the Holy Spirit, who has been given to us" (Romans 5:3-5).

Suffering, whether mental or physical, results in developing perseverance. An Indian proverb states: "He who comes through fire will not faint in the Sun". The strongest trees are not those that grow in heavily protected farms, but those that stand in the open areas where they face the hardships of the weather. Wild animals and birds have to undergo many perils and they are stronger than pet animals and birds. Passing through agony, defeat, failures, obstacles etc. makes one stronger.

While mentioning about the significance of suffering in life, St. Isidore of Seville made this statement: "We should ever be suspicious of our sanctity, if we never meet with any serious obstacle." "The suffering of adversity does not degrade you but exalts you. Human tribulation teaches you; it does not destroy you. The more we are afflicted in this world, the greater is our assurance for the next. The more we sorrow in the present, the greater will be our joy in the future." This is also what Jesus taught through the beatitudes (cfr. Mt. 5:1-2; Lk. 6: 20-23).

As iron is fashioned by fire and on the anvil, so in the fire of suffering and under the weight of trials, our souls receive that form which our Lord desires them to have.

– St. Magdalene Sophie Barat

2.7. Life-giving source

Suffering enables a person to give life to others. Jesus said "Unless a grain of wheat falls into the earth and dies, it remains alone; but if it is dies, it bears much fruit" (Jn.12: 24). A grain of wheat has to suffer in the process of decaying and ends its existence to become life for a plant on which many grains are to be generated. Then these new grains either become a life-giving source directly as food or as seed to give life for a plant to continue the

previous process. In any case sacrifice produces life for others. Donation of human organs before or after death is one way to give life for others. Parents suffer in finding means to feed and fulfill other necessities of their children; in other words dying daily to take care of their children, to keep them alive and for the growth of their children. A similar process is present in the life of a teacher for students, a farmer for his cultivation, a doctor for patients, a soldier for the nation and so on. In these we see that the suffering and sacrifice of someone, gives life and growth for others. Thus suffering also can be a life giving source.

By His sorrowful passion and painful death on the cross Jesus paid the cost to open the gate of eternal life for all humanity - a life-giving source. Jesus the grain of wheat became life-giving bread in the Holy Eucharist. Jesus said "I am the bread of life" (Jn. 6:48) "if anyone eats of this bread, he will live forever" (Jn.6:51). Jesus expects each one of us, carrying our given cross, to pay the price to attain salvation and eternal life for self and others. Thus every one of us can make our daily cross life-giving for our earthly and eternal life.

> *Thy cross, O Lord, is the source of all blessings, the cause of all graces; by it the faithful find strength in weakness, glory in shame, life in death.*
>
> — St. Leo

2.8. Merits promised by Jesus

Jesus promised various rewards; such as conferring of Kingdom of God, sharing of the same table and throne with governing power etc (cfr. Lk. 22: 28-29) for those who are with him in trials. When we reflect on the meaning of these words of Jesus in our context, we understand that rewards will be only for those who stand with him in the midst of trials that occur in our daily life. There is a kind of exclusion of people who run away from sufferings while following Jesus. Rewards are only for those who remain in the battlefield irrespective of hardships. Shareholders who remain in the company even in the midst of painful moments or crisis, have the right to enjoy its profits at the end.

Jesus taught about the reward for those who follow him carrying their own cross and stay with him even in sufferings. In the words of St. Gemma Galgani: "If you really want to love Jesus, first learn to suffer, because suffering teaches you to love." Conferring the kingdom of God is the first promise of Jesus for those who follow him carrying their own cross. Jesus the Son of God has the authority to confer the Kingdom of God to whom He desires. He revealed that eligible candidates for this reward are cross bearers during their earthly span of life. This is similar to his teaching 'enter through the narrow gate that leads to life.'

The second element in the promise of Jesus for closely following him carrying the cross, is a share in His table, "you may eat and drink at my table". This gives us indication that a person who remains with Jesus even in trials will be able to join him in sufferings, and drink his cup. "Can you drink the cup that I drink?" is a question Jesus asked the sons of Zebedee when they expressed their desire to sit with Jesus at His right and left. Secondly being with Jesus in his glory and having meals at his table in the heavenly kingdom is a reward for being with him in following the sacrificial aspect. This is also an answer to those who wish to sit at the right and left of Jesus when He is in glory. The disciples had a dispute for this, though their thought pattern was in the line of the earthly kingdom. Jesus answered the disciples as to who would sit on his right and left when he entered in glory. For us it would mean carrying our daily cross with the attitude demanded by our master to attain the heavenly kingdom. In the context of the Holy Eucharist, it is the people who follow Christ faithfully even in the midst of the trials of daily life, have the right to have the Eucharistic meal from the table of the Lord.

The third promise is a share of power or the entrusting of responsibility. A share of power to rule will be conferred only on those who stand courageously till the end of the battle. During the trials there may be temptations to run away from the battlefield, resulting in not being able to reach the glorious moments and be present at the medal-awarding ceremony. At the starting point of the marathon, many will be there but only a few reach the finishing line. Similarly many are there to begin the race towards perfection but only few reach the destination, since the rest deviate or disappear during the time of hardships.

> *We ought to run after crosses as the miser runs after money. . . Nothing but crosses will reassure us at the Day of Judgment When that day shall come, we shall be happy in our misfortunes, proud of our humiliations, and rich in our sacrifices!*
>
> — St. Jean Marie Baptiste Vianney, the Cure of Ars

2.9. Humility

The sufferings during the time of the trials enable us to be humble and accept our weak human nature. The painful

experiences in our daily life help us to realize better our spiritual poverty and fragility, leading us not to rely totally on our own power, but to turn to God who can give us victory. Human effort is essential for salvation, but this alone will not suffice. We are reminded of this fact through the hurdles of

life faced on our journey towards our destination. The hermits said, 'We become more humbled when we are under trails and temptations, because God, knowing our weakness, protects us. But if we place our trust in our own strength, he takes away his protection and we are lost'. Peter was able to walk on the water as long as his eyes were directed to Jesus, but when this situation changed, he was about to drown in the water and cried out for help, and Jesus had to save him.

Humility is nurtured in the midst of sufferings and grows when provided with essential nourishments. Every stroke we get in our life not only makes us to realize our fragility but also enables us not to be proud of our achievements but give glory to God who is behind our success. Thus daily crosses in a person's life create fertile ground to grow in humility, the mother of all other virtues, a source of God's blessings. Daily crosses in the form of sufferings in our life play the role of an efficient teacher and trainer in practicing humility. Our nothingness is revealed in times of our inability to keep serenity and peace of mind due to various tribulations in our life. The more we undergo sufferings in our life, the more humility we can gain.

> *I prefer to be accused unjustly, for then I have nothing to reproach myself with, and joyfully offer this to the good Lord. Then I humble myself at the thought that I am indeed capable of doing the thing of which I have been accused.*
>
> — St. Therese of Lisieux

2.10.   Share holder in salvation economy

Jesus the Son of God descended on earth, took the form of a human, suffered and died on the cross to save mankind –

the salvific mission of Christ. All those who partake in this mission of Jesus get the benefit of being shareholders in the mission of salvation. His promises in this regard (cfr. Lk. 22: 28-29) ensure that we who stand firm in carrying our daily cross and follow him become sharers in his glory and can even sit on thrones with power. Every suffering patiently endured with the right attitude will count in supporting Jesus' mission, as it has a witnessing value. In the words of St. Paul: "Always carrying in the body the death of Jesus, so that the life of Jesus may also be made visible in our bodies. For while we live, we are always being given up to death for Jesus' sake, so that life of Jesus may be made visible in our mortal flesh" (2 Cor. 4:10-11).

Jesus Christ went through an unjust humiliating suffering on the cross though he was sinless. It is such suffering that separated us from sin. We can participate in his mission of saving mankind when we undergo sufferings and accept them with the attitude of sharing His suffering. Then only can we participate in his glory with happiness (cfr. 1Pet. 4: 12-14). He has opened the door of salvation through the sacrifice of his life on the cross, paying the ransom for humanity. We have to enter by carrying our own cross. In the words of St. Peter, "for to this you have been called, because Christ also suffered for you, leaving you an example, so that you should follow in his steps" (1Pet. 2:21). We have to undergo unjust suffering as our master did during his earthly life. The more we love the cross of Christ and follow in his footsteps, the more can we save our people (cfr. Col.1:24-25). On behalf of the body of Christ, the Church, we have to undergo trials. The ministry entrusted to us will be complete only when we embrace sufferings. Jesus has done his share and we have to continue his mission by our participation and completion in this regard. Our participation in this mission ensures our salvation and that of our fellow brethren too.

> O Christ, I unite my sufferings to yours, my pains with your pains, as I look at your head crowned with thorns.
>
> — St Rafqa Al-Rayes

2.11. More intimacy with God

It is natural that, at the moment of suffering, human beings turn to God for help, especially when all human effort seems futile and God remains as the last resort. Sometimes the doctors give up the treatment of a patient saying that they have done everything they could, and instruct you take the patient home. In other words when all possible medication available has failed, it is natural for us to turn to God. In such a helpless situation even the atheist turns to the retreat centers or pilgrim centers for a cure. And after receiving positive results there, he enters into a deeper union with God, proclaims the blessings of the Almighty, and becomes a vibrant instrument in bringing others for such experiences of God. I have seen a communist leader and atheist in my home town, after he had gone through such an experience of God, becoming leader of a prayer group, and a full-time preacher of God's love, carrying the Bible always and everywhere.

A squirrel once happened to be drowning in the water and someone offered it at a hand. Thereafter this creature never left the person who saved its life from certain death. A similar affection for God can be seen in human beings after an experience of being saved. Charismatic retreat centers have many such testimonies of people coming into closer union with God and religion after certain saving experiences of sufferings. These saving acts can be experienced in many ways for e.g. the cure from sickness, relief at being employed, the birth of a child after long years of waiting, wining a very important court case etc. Thus sufferings in our life enable us to come closer to God and strengthen our intimacy with Him. The life stories of great saints and heroes prove this, showing how they entered into deeper union with God and became His ardent preachers. St. Paul, St. Francis of Assisi and many others belong to this category.

If I were to meet the slave-traders who kidnapped me and even those who tortured me, I would kneel and kiss their hands, for if that did not happen, I would not be a Christian and Religious today... The Lord has loved me so much: we must love everyone... we must be compassionate!

— St. Josephine Bakhita

2.12. Maturity and fruitfulness

A rose plant that has been timely pruned grows better and gives forth more flowers in quality and quantity than the one  which did not have such pruning. The pruning effect is the same in the life of human beings and it is under the plan of God as we read in the scripture; "Every branch that bears fruit he prunes to make it bear more fruit" (Jn. 15:2), "Lord disciplines those whom he loves, and chastises every child whom he accepts" (Heb.12:6). A person attains maturity in the process of facing difficulties and struggles, making him more and more efficient in executing responsibilities and facing the tragic situation in life. The significance of pruning in the spiritual field is well expressed by St. Bernard, "Things cut off sprout forth again, what is drives off returns; therefore the pruning knife should be applied always in the spiritual field."

A plant in the pot, placed on the veranda of a house, faces less adversity and thus has comparatively more secure life. But a plant that grows in the garden has to face the storms, showers, scorching Sun, attack from insects, animals etc.

Comparatively this second category growing in the open air will be better and more fruitful than that which was planted in the pot and placed on the veranda. Children brought up with utmost care, without any freedom even to mingle with their age group, those who have no chance to do any work at home, or do not have training in carrying out responsibilities, will have a dark future as compared to their counterparts who had all the experiences listed above. Experience of poverty, hardship, manual labour, decision making in adverse situation etc., make a person grows better in maturity and fruitfulness even in the adverse life situations. Thus the daily crosses of life in the form of sufferings and struggles to survive are essential for a person to succeed in life. Such personalities will be appreciated and will be in great demand in society. In the words of Sadhu Sunder Singh, "Diamonds do not dazzle with beauty unless they are cut. When they are cut, the rays of the Sun fall on them and make them shine with wonderful colours. So when we are cut into shape by the cross we shine as jewels in the kingdom of God".

The longer the trial to which God subjects you, the greater the goodness in comforting you during the time of trial and in the exaltation after the combat.

– St. Padre Pio of Pietrelcina

Don't Ever Give Up!

Don't ever give up

Failure and Success is in everyone's cup.
Rain becomes more enjoyable
if it follows a sunny day
Food becomes more relishing
if for days hungry you stay
So, don't ever give up

Failure and Success is in everyone's cup.
Gold becomes beautiful ornament,
by moulding and heating
Marble becomes beautiful statues
by carving and beating
So, don't ever give up

Failure and Success is in everyone's cup.
Pebble becomes smooth by constant rolling
A Pencil becomes usable by sharpening
So, don't ever give up

Failure and Success is in everyone's cup.

– Kavitha Krishnamurthy

3

The art of bearing our crosses

When our mental setup is attuned positively towards our daily cross, the weight of our cross will be lighter psychologically, and thereafter we may be able to carry the cross happily even though the physical heaviness of the cross remains the same. Acceptance of the given cross, making our cross of suffering to bear fruit, acquiring strength through the Gethsemane prayer, lightening the burden of the cross by praying for the cross, carrying Jesus along, and faith in his presence, child like trust in God, the Holy Eucharist and its continuity in daily life etc., are means to lighten the weight of our daily cross. These means are explained below in short.

3.1. Acceptance and total surrender

Readiness to accept the given cross and surrender ourselves to the will of God, makes it easy to carry the  cross. Stubbornness and non acceptance increase the heaviness of the cross. We get frustrated and lose peace of mind, whereas our acceptance of the given cross with the understanding that without the knowledge of God nothing happens in our life, helps us to bear the Cross. We should believe that God knows our capacity, and He will not put on us more than we can bear. St. Therese of Child Jesus believed this strongly and said: "Our Lord never asks of us any sacrifice above our strength". Even in the case of temptation and the testing of our faith, God considers our ability to bear. "God is faithful, and he will not let you be tempted beyond your strength, but with the temptation will also provide the way of escape, that you may be able to endure it" (1 Cor. 10:13).

Surrendering to the will of God is what is expected of us and this is also a way to lessen the weight of the Cross, by accepting it positively. Mary did this at the time of the annunciation "Let it be done to me according to your Word" (Lk.1:38), Jesus' surrender to the will of his Heavenly Father can be seen in its climax at Gethsemane "Thy will be done" (Mt. 26:42). St. Ephraim writes, "The potter submits his work to the action of the fire till the clay is hardened. But he is careful not to allow it too little heat, for then the clay will not be sufficiently hard, nor too much heat, for then the clay will be burned and destroyed." God acts like wise. He submits us to the fire of tribulation to the degree necessary to render us more holy; but He will not allow us to be destroyed in the fire.

> *Misfortune is never mournful to the soul that accepts it; for such do always see that in every cloud is an angel's face.*
>
> – St. Jerome

3.2. Enable the cross to bear fruit

Jesus said 'unless a grain of wheat falls into the earth and dies it cannot bear fruit' (cfr. Jn 12; 24). One's attitude towards carrying the cross willed by God can make this act fruitful, or even futile if one carries the cross murmuring and complaining. In a vision Jesus told St. Gertrude: "He who suffers patiently for the love of me that which he is unable to cure, gains a glorious prize."

Since we cannot escape from the cross, we must make it fruitful accepting that this is the will of God for me, thus happily accepting the will of God and making it fruitful for self and others. The first part of the merits is meant to gain blessings, and gain a ticket to heaven for oneself, and the second part of it is useful for others by praying for the welfare of another, offering one's pain. We should remember this at each moment of pain so that our cross bearing is made fruit bearing. In the words of

Edward Hays: "Suffering is like manure; it can be unseemly and offensive, or it can be the "stuff" out of which great productivity comes".

While cleaning our rooms we may find many things useless for us; broken plastic items, iron items, waste papers etc. If we separate them item-wise and sell to the people who in turn take them to the place of recycling, our waste materials will be converted into other new articles and come into the market. Articles useless at a time for us, become useful after going through the proper channels. Similarly our sicknesses, pains of various kinds, appear useless for us, but we can make them useful sources for ourselves and others. If we suffer without complaint, offer them in prayer for our own purification or for a particular intention and conversion of others, they will bear fruit.

When I was in Rome as an assistant parish priest I was given charge of sick people of our parish. While visiting bedridden people I used to hear from them "Father pray for me". I used to answer them, "I shall, but I have a request that you pray for me especially when you are in severe pain because your prayer with pain is more effective than my prayer without any pain". St. Therese of the Child Jesus, who was of the opinion that more souls are saved through suffering than eloquent preaching, exclaimed during her long and painful agony: "The chalice is full to the brim. Never could I have believed it possible to suffer so much . . . I can only find the explanation in my extreme longing to save souls . . . Oh! I would not suffer less."

> *In the same way that a powerful medicine cures an illness, so illness itself is a medicine to cure passion. And there is much profit of soul in bearing illness quietly and giving thanks to God.*
>
> – St. Amma Syncletice

3.3. Importance of Gethsemane

Jesus, who prayed at Gethsemane, got strength and courage to carry the heavy cross, face insults, rebukes, beatings, the embarrassing situation of stripping of his clothes in public etc,. Instead the disciples who were with him slept even though Jesus reminded them to get up and pray so that they may not fall into temptation. They did not go through the real Gethsemane experience. Later when the time of suffering came, the disciples ran away. But Jesus who prayed stood courageously and faced the  suffering unto death leading to the glorious resurrection. In the Bible we get the words of Jesus, "Father, if thou art willing, remove this cup from me; nevertheless not my will but thine, be done." (Lk. 22: 42). Jesus surrendered to the will of his Heavenly Father. I strongly believe Jesus uttered one more sentence "If this is your will give me strength to drink this cup of suffering". In Luke's version we see an angel appeared from heaven and strengthened him' (Lk. 22:43).

In the case of Jesus' public life we see there were two intense spiritual exercises; one in the desert consisting of forty days and the other at Gethsemane. In both cases we see Jesus as the winner; in the first case he defeated Satan and in the second case he defeated the worldly understanding of the cross and suffering, gave his life to save the entire humanity and won a victory over death through his resurrection. Jesus got more spiritual strength through his sacrificial prayer in the desert and praying with agony at Gethsemane. We have to follow the path of Jesus – intense prayer – in confronting sufferings in our life. Our prayer when in agony helps successfully either to remove the suffering, or to get strength to face it. For this we need to surrender to the will of God as Jesus did.

> *If you embrace all things in this life as coming from the hands of God, and even embrace death to fulfill His holy will, assuredly you will die a saint.*
>
> – St. Alphonsus de Liguori

3.4. Praying for the cross

Praying for the cross is an ideal method to lighten the weight of our daily crosses. There are ways and means to make the cross psychologically lighter to carry. The real weight remains but for a mentally easier way to carry the cross, we have to do an exercise previously. Here the method is to pray for the cross. This seems to be a difficult task but it has an effective result in facing the cross in our daily life. If we invite someone, normally we will wait for him or her with proper preparation. It will be the same when  we get information about someone's coming to our home. Instead, a surprise visit may find us unprepared, or lead to an embarrassing situation or sometimes we may not be present at all in the place. In other words precedent knowledge of an event enables us to face the situation with proper mental and physical preparation. If we mentally prepare ourselves to accept sufferings cheerfully for love of God, we can more readily suffer our afflictions.

Similarly if we pray for the cross, sufferings, pains etc, for our purification in whichever form it may appear, we may be prepared to face it. We prayed and so we got it. Let us face it without grumbling or complaint. Mental strength will help us to face it in a proper way and offer the pain or suffering for better merits for oneself and others.

> *If the soul would know the merit which one acquires in temptations suffered in patience and conquered, it would be tempted to say:"Lord, send me temptations.*
>
> — St. Padre Pio of Pietrelcina

3.5. Carrying Jesus along and faith in His presence

Jesus' presence in the boat of the disciples saved their life from the storm (cfr. Mt. 8: 23-27; Mk. 4:35-4; Lk 8: 22-25). On another occasion Jesus' arrival while the disciples were in trouble saved the disciples from the agitation of the waves and the storm. Jesus walked and reached out to them, calmed the wind and restored serenity. (Mt. 14 22-33). Along with the presence of Jesus, faith in his power and request for his help, is also necessary to stand firm in the midst of our struggles. Our life in the world is like a voyage on an ocean. There can be times of peace but  there can also be times of agitation of the waves, storm-like problems in our life too. We have to carry Jesus with us on our life's journey and invoke him with deep faith in his presence and power. This will be an aid to carry our daily cross of sufferings.

Consolation of Jesus in our troubles and adversities can be the source of courage and strength. "Come to me you who are burdened" (Mt. 11:28). Jesus - who healed the sick, gave life to the dead, fed the hungry, drove the evil spirits away, consoled the people in affliction - is our aid in need.

Taking Jesus along with us, wherever we go and in whatever we do, feeling his presence, dialoguing with him through short prayers, enables and strengthens us to face the cross and even get rid of our affliction. "Pray without ceasing" (1 Thes.5:17). 'Lord Jesus Christ have mercy on us' can be a short 'Jesus mantra' on our lips and a life jacket protecting us from dangers.

In the midst of our afflictions, the presence of our Lord is with us, but many of us fail to experience His presence and become frustrated. It is good to reflect once again on the famous story of the foot prints of Jesus in the sand. One night a man had a dream. He dreamed he was walking along the beach with the Lord. Across the sky flashed scenes from his life. For each scene, he noticed two sets of footprints in the sand. One was his and the other was the Lord's. When the last scene of his life flashed before him, he looked back at the footprints in the sand. He noticed that many times along the path of his life there was only one set of foot prints. He also noticed that this happened at the lowest and saddest time in his life. This really bothered him and he questioned the Lord about it, "Lord, you said that once I decided to follow you, you would walk with me all the way. But I notice that during the most troublesome times in my life there is only one set of footprints.' The Lord replied, "My child, I never left you during your time of trial. Where you see only one set of footprints, I was carrying you, the one set was mine".

> *Let us consider what the glorious Virgin endured, and what the holy apostles suffered, and we shall find that they who were nearest to Jesus Christ were the most afflicted.*
>
> — St. Teresa of Jesus

3.6. Child like trust in God

'God knows better' – a conviction and trust of this kind may lighten the weight of the cross. Our knowledge about things we

receive from God, the source of all wisdom and knowledge, is limited. Certainly the source of origin will be greater than the given portion that we all possess. In other words the cause is greater than the effect. Human knowledge is effect and limited, where as God's knowledge is the cause and is unlimited. There is a famous saying that would strengthen us in our afflictions, 'Whatever happened is for our good, whatever is happening is for our good and whatever is going to happen also will be for our good'. We also might have experienced that we make certain future plans for our life, our parents or superior authorities also may have certain plans for each of us, and both these may happen or may not happen. But God has a plan for each one of us (cfr. Jer. 29:11) and this is sure to happen even in the midst of obstacles. Therefore it is better to surrender oneself to God's Will instead of complaining.

Faith and trust in God will enable us to overcome the adversities of our life positively. Our prayers at times are not granted in time or never answered in the way desired. We may get upset and desperate and even stop praying. Only much later we may learn the reason of our requests not being granted. God is our loving father and He knows better what is good for us. We know our past and our present but God knows our past, present and future too. Our demands for certain needs may be harmful for us in the future and knowing this fact our loving Father may not grant our request. A child may stretch his hand to a flame of fire to catch it, but loving parents will not allow the child to do so. The child may cry being prevented in his attempt but later, when older, he will understand why his parents did not allow his action. Similarly God may, even after several requests in prayers, refuse many of our desires which are going to do us harm. We are infants in the sight of God. Our knowledge is very limited when compared to that of our creator. Let us accept our littleness and have a child like trust in God, then our life will become more peaceful and joyful. For children it is enough to trust in their loving parents and obey them. Similarly we should have submission and child like trust in God even in the midst of unfulfilled desires and consequent sufferings. Jesus taught us to have this trust in God the Father (cfr. Mt. 6:25-34; Lk. 12: 22-32).

Let us sing with the psalmist "The Lord is my shepherd: I have everything I need, He lets me rest in fields of green grass and leads me to quiet pools of fresh water. He gives me strength. He guides me in the right paths, as he has promised. Even if I go through the deepest darkness, I will not be afraid, Lord, for you are with me. Your shepherd's rod and staff protect me. I know that your goodness and love will be with me all my life; and your house will be my home as long as I live" (Ps. 23).

> *We must understand then, that even though God doesn't always give us what we want, He always gives us what we need for our salvation.*
>
> — St Augustine

3.7. Holy Eucharist and its continuity in daily life

The Institution of the Eucharist was done by Jesus in the upper room at the last supper. This was a symbolic sacrifice, using wine and bread to symbolize the body and blood of Jesus. And Jesus said, 'Do this in memory of me'. We are following this through our daily Mass as obedient followers of Jesus. It is good and it is very important to follow the command of Jesus daily by celebrating the Holy Eucharist. Did Jesus stop or complete his Eucharistic sacrifice at the upper room? My answer would be 'NO'.

He did not stop nor did He say "The Mass is ended". He continued his journey of sacrifice via Gethsemane, where he got strength for the real/ concrete sacrifice, to Mount Calvary, a place where he sacrificed his life for the entire humanity.

The Mass is not to be ended within the four walls of the church or chapel. It is to be continued through Gethsemane, on the way to Calvary, up to the last concrete sacrifice on the Calvary Mount. Our daily life also, should reflect real sacrifices. If we have to be successful, we need a Gethsemane experience, a deep prayer life, which will give courage and strength to face the temptation and cross of suffering and death.

After the participation of the Holy Eucharist, we are out for our daily affairs where we have to face temptations. These temptations are the testing stones of our continuity of the spirit we have received at the time of the Holy Eucharist. Certainly there may be provoking situations in our life to get angry, temptation to dilute virtuous life for certain favourable gain or pleasures etc. In those circumstances how we maintain the spirit of holiness acquired during the Holy Eucharistic celebration, depends on our understanding of the Holy Eucharist and its continuity in our daily life.

I remember a story narrated by Cardinal Arinze while I was studying at Rome. Once, a priest during Sunday Mass gave a wonderful homily which impressed the entire community and he himself was satisfied that he could give such an impressive sermon. After the Mass while he was wishing the people outside, many praised him about his homily. Meanwhile his servant boy came to him saying, "Father, your brother has just come and is sitting in the refectory. I doubt whether he is your real brother. Please come and meet him". The parish priest with wonder rushed to the refectory because he did not have a brother at all, for his only brother had died two years ago. After seeing a shabby looking person who used to beg on the road side sitting on the chair he shouted: "Get out! Who permitted you to enter in"? Then the beggar said, "You addressed the participants at the Holy Mass as 'brothers and sisters'. You repeated this several times. I thought you meant what you said during the Holy Eucharist. Now I understand that you do not mean what you speak during the Holy Eucharist." The spirit of the Holy Eucharist for that particular priest remained only a few minutes after the Holy Mass. Many lose the grace on their way home itself due to some provoking situation they face and for others at their working place.

> *Oh my Lord! How true it is that whoever works for you is paid in troubles! And what a precious price to those who love you if we understand its value.*
>
> — St. Teresa of Jesus

3.8. Contemplation on the sufferings of Jesus

When we contemplate on the sufferings Jesus underwent for our salvation, we can receive consolation and strength in

our moments of suffering. Though Jesus was sinless, he had to undergo unjust suffering. God the Father willed to use this method for His Son. From birth to death Jesus had to undergo various kinds of sufferings. It is not only on the road to Calvary and on the cross, but throughout his life on the earth, that various humiliations and false accusation were experienced. For each and every suffering we go through, we see a

parallel in the life of Jesus. When we compare in this way, we become aware that we are closely following our master. In the words of St. Teresa of Jesus: "There is no affliction, trial, or labor difficult to endure, when we consider the torments and sufferings which Our Lord Jesus Christ endured for us". We have a master who underwent every form of human suffering, who can sympathize in our suffering. We are sure to get strength and courage by the contemplation of Jesus' sufferings by which our daily crosses can become less weighty. Then easily we can go ahead with our trials and tribulations.

In each of our sufferings we can try to find out whether a similar kind of suffering whether Jesus went through and contemplate on that particular suffering of Jesus. This will enable us to possess a kind of spiritual strength in our painful moments. We notice that Jesus, the Son of God, though sinless, for our sake went through such an agonizing moment. Then we sinful human beings can consider beneficial and acceptable, certain purification through suffering. Blessed Joan Antidea Thouret very well expressed: "I am a sinner, and I consider myself very fortunate to suffer something for the name of Jesus Christ". Through our sufferings we can follow Jesus on the road to Calvary, and remain under the cross of Jesus to witness his unjust suffering and death on the cross, and prove our loving intimacy with him. This kind of contemplation will ease our pain and make us ready to accept any kind of suffering in our life.

> If you seek patience, you will find no better example than the cross. . . Christ endured much on the cross, and did so patiently, because when he suffered he did not threaten; he was led like a sheep to the slaughter and he did not open his mouth.
>
> — St. Thomas Aquinas

3.9. Wise and mature spiritual director

A wise and mature spiritual director can be an aid to a soul during the suffering moments, so as not to lose hope and trust in God. Here the terms wise and mature are used, because not everybody can become a genuine spiritual director to guide a person during his painful moments. First of all a spiritual director should be highly spiritual and trustworthy in this regard to handle the situation with proper guidance. If we can't find such a reliable person

around, it would be better to avoid approaching anybody just for the sake of consultation. Instead we can rely on Jesus, a true model and guide. Through prayer and contemplation we can get necessary help in our struggles. Thus St. Ignatius of Loyola prayed: "Teach us, Good Lord, to give and not count the cost; to fight and not to heed the wounds; to toil and not to seek for rest; to labor and not to ask for any reward save that of knowing that we do thy will".

An experienced saintly spiritual director, who has gone through various struggles in life and reached spiritual heights by ascetical practices, can enlighten the persons groping in the darkness of trials. A good spiritual director can guide a person in dilemma to take right decisions. He can instill hope in them in the midst of adversities, and empower them to face the trials, temptations, physical or mental agony, accusations etc. Thus carrying our daily crosses, willed by God for our betterment, will become easy and profitable.

> *All those who unjustly inflict upon us tribulations, anguish, shame and injuries, sorrows and torments, martyrdom and death, are our friends whom we ought to love much, because we shall gain eternal life by those things which they make us suffer.*
>
> — St. Francis of Assisi

3.10. Ascetical practices

Ascetical practices can strengthen a person to face any kind of trials. Practices like unceasing prayer, mortification, penances,

fasting, abstinence etc. can strengthen a person spiritually to embrace any sufferings that come in his/ her daily life. A spiritually strengthened person will be always waiting to get sufferings to be purified and to follow Jesus more closely, even embracing sufferings as Jesus did. Ascetical practices also will protect, safeguard and enable us to go through physical or mental pain in our life through interior vigilance. Once someone asked Abba Agathon about bodily asceticism and he replied: "Man is like a tree, bodily asceticism is the foliage, interior vigilance the fruit."

Unceasing prayer (cfr.1Thes. 5:17) enables us to get unceasing strength to carry our daily cross. The presence of Jesus is felt in our daily cross. This prayer can give strength in carrying our daily crosses. Simon of Cyrene was compelled to carry his cross for a short time (cfr. Mk. 15: 21). The "Jesus prayer" we recite in our minds unceasingly would enable us to feel Jesus' presence in and around us always. It's a strong helping aid to carry our cross of sufferings. Our fasting, abstinences, bodily mortifications of various kinds, strengthen us spiritually to face any painful situation. Physically we may become weak but our inner spiritual strength will be strong to face any adversities. A spiritually strengthened person will not react against accusations or criticism. He will not be desperate in times of agony.

> *The Cross will not crush you; if its weight makes you stagger, its power will also sustain you.*
>
> — St. Padre Pio of Pietrelcina

3.11. Bearing it for the love of Jesus

A person doesn't mind going through hardship and pain to achieve his/her goal, or when it is the case of a service for

his/her beloved. It is a fact that a person goes even to the extreme point of suffering to express his love towards his beloved. Then the burden of carrying the cross is not felt so keenly. The readiness to bear the cross for the other increases in the measure he/she loves the beneficiary. Here pain is converted into love and is not felt at all. Even at the time of severe pain a person will be able to shed tears of joy. It is believed that at the time of giving birth to a child, in the midst of pain, the inner disposition of a mother is happiness at the thought of seeing her newborn baby.

In general a person will be ready to undergo any inconveniences and discomfort for the sake of the betterment of his/her beloved. This same disposition will not exist in the case of an outsider. A mother may be seen washing or cleaning with affection the dirt caused by her own child, whereas her disposition may vary when doing similar work for other children. Service can be rendered with utmost love to our own bedridden kith and kin. But there is an absence of that affection in many cases when the same service is carried out as a duty with payment. Love for a person overcomes the pain and discomfort experienced in executing certain services.

The cross borne with the disposition that it is being done for the love of Jesus, enables us to bear it joyfully. The depth of our love for Jesus turns our hardships into happiness and a readiness to endure the extreme side of suffering. The more we love Jesus, the more will we be able to suffer for him. Our love for Jesus takes away the weight of our cross and makes it very light to carry. Thus the realization that our sufferings on earth are meant only to follow Jesus very closely on the way towards eternal life, lessens our burden in bearing them. If we reach a deeper love and intimacy with Jesus, we will be able to say with St. Paul, "Who will separate us from the love of Christ? Will hardship, or distress, or persecution, or famine or nakedness, or peril, or sword? ... For I am convinced that neither death nor life, nor angels, nor rulers, nor things present, nor things to come, nor powers, nor height, nor depth, nor anything else in all creation, will be able to separate us from the love of God in Christ Jesus our Lord." (Rom. 8:35-39).

Together with the love of Jesus we need to be aware of the result of this love, namely his presence and protection. We need to feel the presence of Jesus in the suffering which we endure for the sake of his love. This sense of divine presence gives us strength and courage to bear our crosses. We have a person with us who underwent all kinds of human sufferings in his attempt to save mankind from the bondage of sin. Our love for Jesus will enable us to feel less the burden of the cross, and will strengthen us, make us courageous and finally help us to bear our sufferings with joy.

> *He who wishes to love God does not truly love Him if he has not an ardent and constant desire to suffer for His sake.*
>
> – St. Aloysius Gonzaga

3.12. Praise and thanksgiving

The realization that our sufferings are for our betterment enables us to praise and thank God for His love for us.

When we praise and thank God during our sufferings, we do not feel their burden or bitterness. It helps us forget our pain, leading us to rejoice in our agony. The Apostles had happiness in their sufferings; "As they left the court, they rejoiced that they were considered worthy to suffer dishonor for the sake  of the name" (Act. 5:41). The martyrs of the early centuries were loud in praising and thanking God even in the midst of fire and lions waiting to devour them. They were able to sing joyfully when the adversaries in turn were waiting to see their death and enjoy their cries. Some of them miraculously came out untouched by fire or the hungry wild animals. Martyrs happily underwent tortures for the love of Christ and they shouted praise and thanks during the severe torments. St. Polycarp of Smyrna, St. Justin, St. Cecilia, St. Agatha and St. Lawrence of Rome are some of those who embraced persecution joyfully in this way.

Praise and thanks in times of suffering also bring down an inner healing for us, and the ability to forgive our adversaries who caused us pain. Thus the medicinal effect of praise and thanks in painful moments enables us to bear sufferings courageously. Secondly, there is an evangelization effect of praise and thanks at the time of sufferings. In our agonizing moments we have to thank and praise God in order to lessen the burden and joyfully embrace our crosses. This brave action can also be a testimony of our love for Jesus, and thus bring many other souls closer to Jesus. There are such incidents of praise and thanks of suffering souls in the midst of their bodily pain, that have resulted in the conversion of the persecutors, making them in turn ardent followers of Jesus Christ. Our joy will be doubled as we become instruments to increase the faith of the others in Jesus. In this way the benefits of our sufferings rise higher in degree as we praise and thank God in times of sufferings.

I thank God for this illness and these physical discomforts, because I have the time to converse with the Lord Jesus.

— St. Faustina Kowalska

Take Heart and Wait

If but one message I may leave behind,
One single word of courage for my kind,
It would be this — Oh, brother, sister, friend,
Whatever life may bring —
what God may send,
No matter whether clouds
lift soon or late —
Take heart and wait!

Despair may tangle darkly at your feet,
Your faith dimmed, and hope,
once cool and sweet,
Be lost — but suddenly above a hill,
A heavenly lamp, set on a heavenly sill
Will shine for you and point the way to go,
How well I know

For I have waited through the dark, and I
Have seen a star rise in the blackest sky
Repeatedly — it has not failed me yet.
And I have learned God never will forget
To light his Lamp — if we but wait for it,
It will be lit.

— Gracve Noll Crowell

Conclusion

Without loss there is no gain, without paying the higher price we can't get an object with higher value. A lazy student gets bad results but a student who sacrifices even his leisure time for study, gets good results after the exam. A lazy farmer who never goes to the field after sowing the seed is disappointed while harvesting, whereas a farmer who spends more time in the field and gives his whole effort for a better crop is glad while harvesting. Gold is purified in the fire and a just man is perfected on the cross of suffering and pain. Avoiding the cross is equal to rejecting the heavenly reward after life on earth. Remember the words of Jesus: 'Enter through the narrow gate to reach eternal life' (Mt. 7:14). Creating a positive attitude towards carrying the cross of suffering and the Grace of God acquired through prayers can give one cheerfulness to carry the cross and also a reward for the same. Otherwise we may go on in life carrying the cross with much pain and without a reward. Suffering is a part of human life and no one can avoid it totally; then why do we not make it profitable in our life? Recycling the moments of pain in a productive manner can make them useful for us and others.

To gain eternal life, the cross is the surest way and without the cross no one can be a Christian, "Go where you like, search where you will; neither above nor below, can one find a more sure way than the way of the cross" (Imitation, 2, 12).

> *You must learn to love suffering, our Lord gives his crown of thorns to his friends. Seek nothing better. I am happier in my bed with a crucifix, than a queen on her throne.*
>
> — St. Marie Bernadette Soubirous

God gives me More than I ask

I asked God for strength that I may achieve;
I was made weak, that I might
learn humbly to obey.

I asked for health that
I may do great things;
I was given infirmity,
that I might do better things.

I asked for riches, that I might be happy;
I was given poverty, that I might be wise.

I asked for power, that I might
have the praise of men;

I was given weakness, that I might
feel the need of God.

I asked for all things,
that I might enjoy life;
I got nothing that I asked for —
but everything I hoped for.

Almost despite myself,
my unspoken prayers were answered.
I am among all men, most richly blessed.

– Anon

Other books of the same author

Price of a Precious Pearl : Religious Poverty lived and taught by Bl. Mother Teresa of Culcutta, ISPCK, Delhi, 2009

Cross and Mission: Challenges and Priorities in Evangelisation among the Indigenous People of North India, ISPCK, Delhi, 2010.

The Religious World of the Bhils, ISPCK, Delhi, 2011.

Carrying the Cross and Following Jesus: The Significance and art of Bearing our Crosses, Shanti Ashram, Sagar, 2015.

Jesus, Abode of Mercy: Tips for our Daily Living from the Life and Teaching of Jesus, ISPCK, Delhi, 2016.

Obedience, ISPCK, Delhi, 2017.